MY LITTLE PONY

UNICORN SLEEPOVER

Farshore

First published in Great Britain 2023 by Farshore
An imprint of HarperCollins*Publishers*
1 London Bridge Street, London SE1 9GF
www.farshore.co.uk

HarperCollins*Publishers*
Macken House, 39/40 Mayor Street Upper,
Dublin 1, D01 C9W8, Ireland

Licensed by:

Hasbro

MY LITTLE PONY and HASBRO and all related trademarks and
logos are trademarks of Hasbro, Inc. ©2023 Hasbro.

ISBN 978 0 0085 9658 3
Printed in the United Kingdom
001

A CIP catalogue record for this title is available from the British Library.

MEET THE PONIES!

SUNNY

PIPP

ZIPP

OPALINE

izzy

Misty

Ever since she had moved to Maretime Bay, Izzy the Unicorn had felt different. She loved her friends, Sunny, Hitch, Zipp and Pipp, but it was lonely not having any Unicorn friends in town.

Sometimes she missed Bridlewood, the land of the Unicorns, where she grew up.

One day, Izzy was out walking with little Sparky, Hitch's baby dragon, when she noticed a new Unicorn called Misty had arrived in town. Izzy was sure they were going to be best friends!

Misty was a bit shy, so Izzy wanted to make her feel welcome. She had an idea that would help her feel right at home in no time.

"I know!" said Izzy, "Let's have a traditional Unicorn sleepover tonight! You can meet all my friends at the Crystal Brighthouse and we'll have the best time ever!"

"Oh, tonight? I'm not sure …" Misty began.
But Izzy was already rushing off to organise
the big night before Misty could refuse.

Misty wasn't who Izzy thought she was. She was really a spy for Opaline, an evil Alicorn pony. Opaline wanted to steal all the pony magic in Equestria!

Misty galloped back to Opaline's castle to tell her about Izzy's invite.

"You should go to the sleepover and trick the ponies into thinking you're their friend," Opaline said. "Then you can steal Sunny's precious magic lantern and their powers will be ours!"

Opaline laughed wickedly. Misty gulped; she wasn't so sure this was a good idea.

Back at the Crystal Brighthouse, Izzy couldn't wait to tell her friends all about Misty and her amazing sleepover plans.

Izzy's friends were happy to help her get ready for the big night and they were excited to get to know Misty.

"This is going to be the best sleepover anypony has ever been to in all of Equestria!" gasped Izzy, who was bursting with excitement.

There was a lot to do to get ready for the sleepover.

Zipp strung up beautiful twinkling lights.

Sunny and Pipp hung up colourful decorations.

Soon enough, the doorbell
chimed. It was Misty at the door.

Izzy had so many plans. She wanted to make sure everypony had a fun night.

First they crafted paper Unicorn horns and decorated them with glitter and gems.

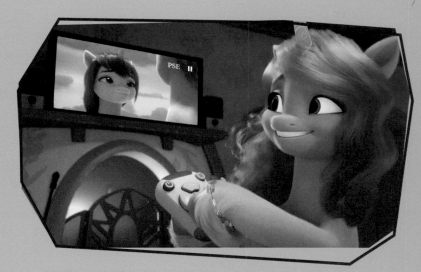

Then they made a giant tower of cushions.

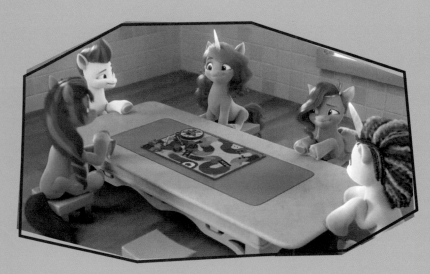

Then they played board games.

Then they watched a movie.

And it wouldn't be a sleepover without snacks of course! All the ponies happily munched on chocolate ponycorn and bowls of sweet treats.

Misty hadn't been able to find the magic lantern, but she was surprised to discover she was really enjoying herself. These ponies were actually pretty cool.

But as the night went on, Zipp became a little suspicious of Misty.

Misty didn't seem to know anything about all the Unicorn traditions Izzy talked about.

And when Izzy wanted to do a Unicorn sing-along, Misty didn't know any of the words to the famous Bridlewood Unicorn song.

"Erm, nowhere ... I, um ..." Misty blushed. "I better be going now actually!"

"Wait, don't leave Misty!" Izzy pleaded. But Misty had already dashed out the door before Izzy could stop her.

"My sleepover has been a total disaster!" Izzy cried.

"Don't worry Izzy, I know things didn't go as you planned but the night's not over yet," said Sunny, trying to cheer her up.

"Yeah, we can still have fun!" added Pipp.

"That's OK," Izzy sighed, "a traditional Unicorn sleepover isn't the same when it's not in Bridlewood anyway. Sometimes I miss home so much and I thought having Misty here would help. But now she's gone!"

Izzy started tidying away the sleepover things. She felt miserable and missed home even more now.

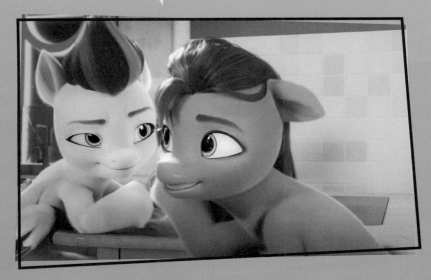

Sunny had an idea that she hoped would cheer Izzy up. She asked Zipp to distract Izzy while she and Pipp quietly snuck off.

"Come on," she whispered to Pipp, "Let's bring a little bit of Bridlewood to the Brighthouse!"

Together, the two friends decorated the bedroom to look like Bridlewood. They draped strings of gems from the ceiling and placed twinkling crystals all over the room.

They dimmed the lights and the magic lantern shone a pattern on the walls that made the room look like a forest. It was magical.

"Surprise!" cheered Sunny, as Izzy trotted into the bedroom.

"Wow! It looks just like home," gasped Izzy. She gazed around the room, amazed. "And this is some pretty impressive crafting too – maybe you all have a bit of Unicorn in you after all!" Izzy giggled.

Even though the sleepover hadn't gone quite as planned, the friends still had a pony-riffic night. They hadn't worked out who Misty really was – but that was a mystery for another day!